unplugged

To Aiden, Annie, and Eli

Library of Congress Cataloging-in-Publication Data

Names: Antony, Steve, author, illustrator.
Title: Unplugged / by Steve Antony.
Description: First American edition. | New York: Scholastic Press,
an imprint of Scholastic Inc., 2018. | Summary: Blip is always plugged into
her computer—until one day a blackout forces her outdoors, and she
discovers that the real world is a lot more interesting than she realized.
Identifiers: LCCN 2016059278 | ISBN 9781338187373 (jacketed hardcover)
Subjects: LCSH: Computers and children—Juvenile fiction.
CYAC: Computers—Fiction. |Classification: LCC PZ7.A632 Un 2018
DDC [E]—dc23 LC record available at https://lccn.loc.gov/2016059278

10 9 8 7 6 5 4 3 2 1   18 19 20 21 22

Printed in China 54

This edition first printing, March 2018

Unplugged

Steve Antony

Scholastic Press • New York

Blip liked being plugged
into her computer.

On her computer . . .

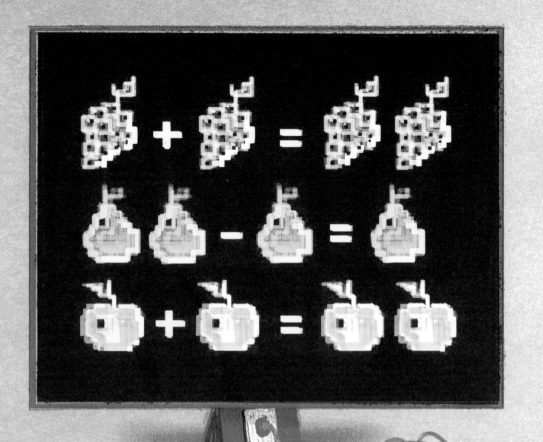

Blip learned
new things,

played fun games,

danced to music,

and visited
faraway places...

all day long.

But one day...

there was a BLACKOUT!

And Blip tripped over her wire!

She tumbled...

all the way...

downstairs...

and out the front door.

Blip toppled
down a steep, grassy hill,

rolled through a forest of very tall trees,

and drifted down a long, winding river.

Blip was outside.

Outside, Blip learned new things,

played fun games,

danced to music,

and visited
faraway places...

all day...

long.

But it was getting late.

Blip sailed back up the long, winding river,

and walked back through the forest of very tall trees,

and climbed back
up the steep,
grassy hill...

where she said good-bye
to her new friends.

upstairs...

all the way...

Blip walked...

and plugged back
into her computer.

Blip liked being plugged into her computer.
But all she could think about . . .

was how great it was . . .

to be . . .

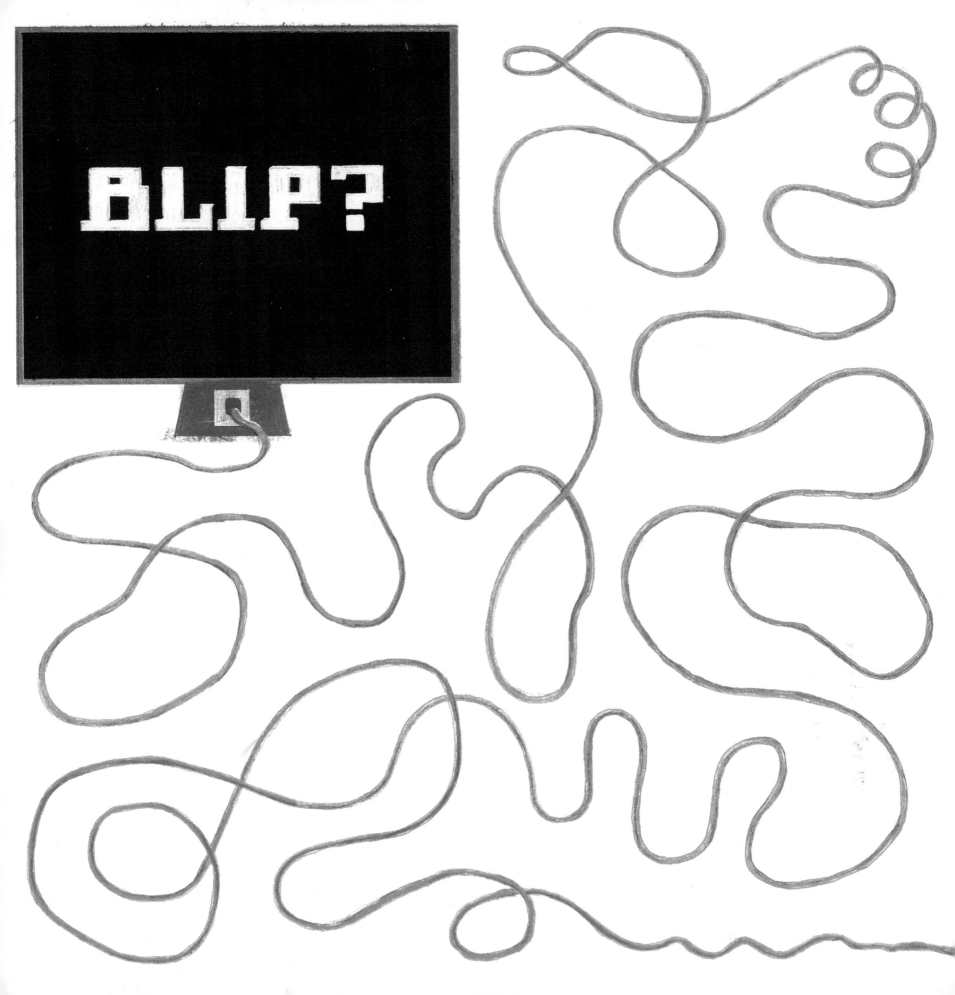